The Raven Calls

THE Raven Calls

Davis Endava

 Black Bears & Blueberries Publishing

ISBN 979-8-9902038-0-8

Cover illustration by Lily Abrams
Book design by Paul Nylander | Illustrada

Published by Black Bears & Blueberries Publishing
Duluth, Minnesota
www.blackbearsandblueberries.com

A Native owned non-profit publishing company, with a focus on creating and developing Native children's books for all young people written by Native writers and illustrated by Native artists.

This book is dedicated to Vashon Island,
to its known and unknown histories,
and to all the kids who feel a bit adrift,
seeking a connection to their heritage.

*S*plash! The rock made a cheerful sound as it took a joyful dive into the sparkling blue water. Raven grinned, her eyes tracing the playful ripples that danced away from the center. Eager for more fun, she leaned down to snatch another rock, this time a shiny red one. With determination shining in her eyes, she pulled her arm back and swung it with all the strength she could muster. Another delightful "Plop!" echoed, this time farther away.

Meet Raven, a spirited young girl who called Vashon Island home, nestled in the gentle waters of the Puget Sound. She belonged to the indigenous people of the place, a community deeply connected to the island and its surroundings for countless generations. Raven's days were filled with the magic of the outdoors—playing among the trees, frolicking on the beaches, and soaking in the wonders of the south Salish Sea ecosystems.

Recently, her parents had lovingly passed on the ancient art of fishing and gathering shellfish along the island's shoreline, a tradition carried through centuries by their ancestors.

Raven was captivated by the wisdom and skills her parents shared, noting the joy that sparkled in their eyes when they cast nets to capture the swift salmon. Entranced by their teachings, Raven made the shoreline her second home, practicing the art of fishing as often as she could. In addition to her coastal adventures, she adored her Nintendo Switch Pokemon game, sang melodies that echoed through the island, climbed trees with unmatched agility, explored hidden treasures, skipped rocks with precision, and transformed bits of nature into beautiful pieces of art.

This sunny Sunday, Raven found herself at the water's edge, eager to perfect her net-fishing skills. As she stood there, the rhythmic ripples on the surface of the water and the soothing sounds of the waves embraced her. Today was dedicated to mastering the art of net-fishing, and Raven was armed with her trusty fishing net, a sturdy rope, and a small bucket for her potential catch. Just in case, she brought along her cherished Nintendo Switch, carefully secured in a dry bag tucked amidst the shore's rocks.

Raven took a deep breath and stepped into the cool water. She waded out a little ways, feeling the soft sand squish beneath her toes. She unfurled her net, examining the mesh carefully to make sure there were no tears or holes. Once satisfied, she began to practice her technique. With a grin on her face, she unfurled her fishing net, its mesh sparkling in the sunlight. But, oh, the first few throws were a bit of a mess. The net rebelled, tangling and folding in on itself as if it had a mind of its own. Raven sighed and had to start over more than once. Frustration began to creep into her mind, like a little storm cloud on a sunny day.

As she felt that frustration, something interesting happened. Her heart raced a little faster, and her cheeks flushed with a mix of determination and annoyance. Raven could feel the energy building up inside her, like a pot about to boil over. But she didn't let it take control. Instead, she took a moment to breathe and looked closely at the water, like a detective on a mission. Studying the playful dance of the waves, Raven noticed how the water moved and swirled. It was like a puzzle waiting to be solved. With each throw, she adjusted her angle and pitch, trying to match the rhythm of the sea. It wasn't easy, and sometimes the net still rebelled, but Raven kept at it. She turned her frustration into a challenge, determined to lean into the dance between her net and the water.

Gradually, Raven began to get the hang of it. She found her rhythm, and her throws became smoother and more confident. She tossed the net out with a flick of her wrist, watching as it spread wide and sank down into the water. Then, with a swift yank, she pulled the rope back towards her, imagining the weight of the fish she hoped to catch. As the afternoon wore on, Raven continued to practice, each throw more precise than the last. She didn't catch a fish, but she smiled to herself, proud of her skill, and weary from the hours of practice.

Turning towards the shore, she noticed a group of tourists taking photos of her as they were shellfishing. Raven froze. She really disliked being taken pictures of, especially when people don't ask. Also, she didn't know much about her people's history, but she did know that her people still had their rights to fish and gather shellfish in their traditional places around Vashon's shore-lines. She knew that tourists definitely didn't have those rights. She had learned about the Medicine Creek Treaty in school, where members of the Salish Sea tribes ceded nearly all of their lands to the United States in 1854. Raven knew that her people had been forced to leave their ancestral homeland and move to another tribe's reservation, where most of their descendants still lived in the Tacoma area. Only a few, like Raven, still lived on Vashon island. The tribe had kept three small reservations, and access to all their traditional hunting and fishing grounds. But she didn't know the stories. Her parents had worked hard to fit into the overarching American culture because they felt like it would be safer for their children. Later in Raven's life, they tried to take Raven to pow-wows, have her learn from the elders and show her the reservation. At that point, Raven just didn't feel much connection. She would say, "Mom, Dad, we're just like everyone else! I don't understand why you're trying to make me feel different."

Raven did enjoy hearing the little tidbits of stories that her parents shared with her though. They talked about animals and plants in their area and how they're linked to their ancestors. It made her feel amazing, like she was part of something big and connected to the world around her. She loved learning about how to fish with nets. She was always curious about her identity, and these stories and skills sparked her interest. However, fully embracing her ancestors was a different story. It was tough for her to connect with it because it felt overwhelming and unfamiliar, especially living on Vashon Island. It's not like she had a lot of people around her who were like her, and that can feel isolating sometimes.

But now, Raven felt her heart sink, and her face warm when she saw the tourists taking the beautiful shellfish from their homes. She wanted to go up to them and tell them about the Medicine Creek Treaty, and the rights of the shellfish to live undisturbed. She thought about those more-than-human beings scared in their shells. There were fewer of these beings than ever, because people had been taking all the shellfish they saw to eat, and weren't leaving any so they may grow. Her mom had taught her how to fish with respect for the animals, giving each one love as they picked them up. She remembered her mom telling her to leave five shellfish for every one she picked up. She knew that many people were not aware of this. Her voice caught in her throat.

As the tourists walked away, still taking shellfish and photos, she looked down frustrated and confused. She hadn't felt her body react in that way before; the warm cheeks, the sinking heart. She sighed, and squished the mud between her toes. As she walked towards the shore, she tried to shake off the feeling, but it just wouldn't go away. So, she did what she always did when she needed to clear her head - she kicked at the slick rocks, watching them fly out and collide with the water, creating satisfying splashes. The rhythmic sound of the waves lapping at the shore helped calm her racing thoughts, but it was the skipping stones that brought a smile back to her face. She was delighted by the ripples she could make. Looking down, she picked out a flat stone to jump on the surface of the water. *One, two, three . . .* she counted as it skipped. Raven reached down and picked up another stone, feeling its smoothness in her hand. She took a deep breath and let it out slowly, then skipped the stone across the water. It bounced a few times before sinking into the depths below. Raven repeated the action, focusing on the way the stone skipped and bounced. It was a simple pleasure, but it was enough to distract her from the frustration she felt towards the tourists. She skipped stone after stone, lost in thought and the repetitive motion. Her eyes flickered down to find another one, when they landed upon a small, shimmering red clay rock. As she picked it up, she felt a strange energy flow through her body.

Whoooosh, suddenly the wind picked up around Raven, startling her and making her bones go cold. She held tighter onto the stone. *Whoooosh,* the wind flew through her hair. *Whoooooosh* it made ripples across the water. Raven felt her throat tighten again, her jaw clenched and she dropped the stone. The wind stopped. She looked around on the beach to see if anyone else had seen what just happened. With wide eyes, Raven scanned the shoreline, half-expecting to see a curious onlooker who had witnessed the wind's dance. To her relief— or perhaps disappointment—no human observers lingered; just the shellfish and the seagulls. She knew the wind could be unpredictable on Vashon Island, but this felt different. It was like the wind was alive, like it had a purpose. She shook her head, trying to dispel the thought. It was silly, wasn't it? But as Raven looked down at the stone, laying simply on the ground, she couldn't shake the feeling that something had shifted. It shimmered in the daylight as if it had the stars sparkling inside of it. Inhaling deeply, she bent over and touched the stone with her fingertip. Suddenly she could hear a whisper in her ear.

"Pick me up," it said. *"Keep me safe, you'll know why soon."*

She felt a certainty come over her, and she did just that. Picking up the red rock, she felt the whispers of the wind around her. It felt strange, but comforting this time. She lay the stone in her pocket and felt the air settle.

In Raven's cozy room, soft yellow curtains swayed gently in the breeze from the open window, allowing the crisp evergreen scent of the Puget Sound through. She was on the second story of the house, and a cedar tree swayed out her window. Moonlight danced across the walls, casting shadows of her potted plants onto the floor. A shelf filled with books about animals and nature stood beside her bed, alongside a colorful display of Pokémon figurines. Her Nintendo Switch rested on a small table, ready for a quick game before bedtime. On her bedspread, colorful images of birds and trees brought a touch of the outdoors inside.

That night, before she went to bed, Raven held the smooth stone in her hand, marveling at its intricate patterns and cool touch. It seemed to hum with energy, filling her with a sense of wonder. As she carefully tucked it under her pillow, a gentle breeze rustled through her room once more, lifting the edges of her clothes. It felt as though the stone was connecting her to something ancient and powerful, and she couldn't help but feel a tingling sense of excitement as she settled into bed for the night. Snuggling up with her favorite stuffed animal, a little orca whale, her eyes fluttered closed and her mind wandered into sleep.

Whoosh, suddenly the air picked up around her again. *Whooooosh*, Raven felt her body lift out of her bed. *Whooooooooooooosh*, the wind surrounded her, and on its current she was softly carried out the window. Raven's heart was racing as she found herself lifted off her bed and carried out the window on the gusts of wind. She felt weightless, her body suspended in midair as she was surrounded by the swirling currents. The wind howled in her ears, drowning out all other sounds.

Peering down at the distant ground below, Raven's stomach churned with a blend of fear and excitement. She had always been nervous about heights, and now, with nothing but the wind to support her, her anxiety spiked. Then, she remembered something her teacher had told her: to tap on both sides of her body when she felt anxious because it helped both sides of her brain connect again. As she looked out at the beautiful night and took a deep breath, her anxiety started to still. The rhythmic tapping and the calming night air helped her find a sense of peace amidst the nervousness. The wind swirled in patterns, catching the nighttime fog as it danced. As she floated through the night sky, Raven couldn't help but marvel at the fog. It swirled and twisted, coming together to create a breathtaking tapestry that stretched out before her. She felt as though she was flying through a painting, the colors and shapes blurring together as she was swept along by the wind. Finally, the wind began to calm, and Raven felt herself being gently lowered to the ground. She landed softly, her bare feet sinking into the damp muddy earth. Looking down, she saw that the fog had created a path before her, a winding trail of still, misty air that stretched off into the distance.

Puzzled, Raven's heart began to beat quickly. Suddenly, she felt a weight deposit in her pocket. Curiously, she reached in and found the red rock. As her fingers touched its smooth surface, she felt the wind respond around her. Raven's heart settled as she recognized the rock; by now, she had grown to love it. With the familiar weight in her pocket, she felt a sense of calm wash over her. Looking up at the cedar tree beside her second-story window, she sighed. Then, she turned her gaze back to the foggy pathway below, admiring its intricate designs. The surrounding trees towered above her, their branches gently swaying in the wind. Taking a breath, she could smell the salty air of the Puget Sound. She put one foot in front of the other, stepping barefoot silently and slowly on the soil. The evergreen trees rustled around her as she walked, as if to welcome her to this part of the island. Salmonberry bushes snagged at her clothes when she stepped too close, as if to give her a plant's kiss.

Sometimes, Raven would feel the prick of a nettle sting. Her mother had told her that their tribal people had used nettles to make rope, medicine, and delicious nettle poppers over the fire.

Raven followed the trail of fog as it led her down a steep hill. Sometimes when she stepped, she would slide, reaching out to grasp onto an alder or vine maple to steady herself. She weaved in the woods until the path flattened out, and opened up to a cliff with a viewpoint of the water, dappled in moonlight. In the center of the grassy field there was a massive, ancient cedar tree. The tree was enormous, with a trunk so wide that it would take ten people to encircle it. Its branches reached out thickly across the sky, as if it was trying to reach the stars. As Raven stood beside the cedar tree, she felt a pull toward its rough bark and fragrant leaves. She longed to reach out and connect with the wisdom it held. With a sense of reverence, she placed her hand on the bark, feeling its strength and resilience beneath her fingertips. Then, unable to resist, she plucked a few cedar leaves and tasted them, savoring their sharp, refreshing flavor. Her mother's words echoed in her mind as she savored the taste. She remembered the stories of their people, how cedar had been used for generations as a powerful medicine. From soothing painful joints to easing coughs and fevers, cedar held a wealth of healing properties. And beyond its medicinal uses, cedar was also seen as a protector, its purifying smoke used to ward off negative energies. As Raven breathed in the scent of the cedar and felt its energy envelop her, she understood why it held such significance for her people. It wasn't just a tree; it was a symbol of resilience, healing, and protection—a connection to her ancestors and the land they cherished.

As Raven stood beside the cedar tree, she felt the red rock in her pocket warm, as if urging her to pick it up. Curious, she drew it out and held it in her hand, watching as it sparkled in the moonlight. The wind whooshed around her, as if in response to the rock's energy. As Raven moved closer to the tree, she noticed something extraordinary. The rock twinkled with more depth, and as she examined it closely, intricate star constellations appeared on its surface. Her eyes widened in wonder as she traced the patterns with her fingertips.

As the wind picked up, Raven felt its force pushing her gently towards the cedar tree. She stood there for a moment, leaning against the wind, feeling its power surrounding her. And then, with a sense of trust and surrender, she released herself into the wind's embrace. It guided her arm effortlessly, as if knowing exactly where she needed to go. As she carefully put the rock on a low branch, she felt a surge of energy, as if the tree was responding to her gesture. The wind picked up, rustling the leaves and filling the air with a sweet, earthy scent. She closed her eyes and took a deep nervous breath, feeling the earth beneath her feet and the rustling of the evergreens around her. When she opened her eyes, she noticed that the tree was glowing with a soft, pulsing light. And then she heard it: a soft voice, almost like a whisper, calling her name. Startled but curious, Raven turned towards the tree, searching for the source of the voice. But all she could see was the red rock, gleaming in the moonlight. She reached out to touch it, and as her fingers brushed its surface, she felt a sudden jolt of electricity, as if she had been plugged into the earth itself. And then the voice spoke again, clearer this time:

"*Raven,*" the voice said. "*You are a daughter of the tribal people of this land, and your roots are deep in the earth, rooted to the rocks and boulders beneath us. Find me, and I'll tell you the stories."*

Panting, she woke up in a sweat. Quickly, she reached under her pillow and felt for the red rock. It was still there. Raven thought back to what had just happened.

"The pathway, and the hill," she murmured, "the rock, and the tree . . ." Raven felt jittery, and her mind felt very foggy. She shook her head to try to clear her thoughts. Raven knew she needed to see the tree again. She knew it was important. She also didn't know if the tree was real, or if it was just in her dreams. Either way, she figured she needed to write down what she saw. Fumbling, she rushed through her drawers to find a piece of paper. Pausing, she took a shaky breath. She wanted to do this right. She closed her eyes to try to recreate the patterns hidden in the foggy pathway in her mind. Raven knew it was important to take her time and make them as similar to her dreams as she could. Slowly, she drew the lines of the trail, and the weaving designs inside.

Raven ran downstairs to the kitchen, where her mom and siblings were eating breakfast.

"Honey," her mother called to Raven, "would you like some cereal?"

Raven nodded distractedly as her youngest brother, Kai, ran over with a bowl of Lucky Charms, his excitement palpable. He was always eager to help out, and Raven couldn't help but smile at his enthusiasm. She quickly shoveled food into her mouth, eager to finish her breakfast so she could go explore the dream she had experienced. In the background, the TV blasted ThunderCats Roar cartoons, providing entertainment for her siblings. Meanwhile, her dad raced downstairs in his mechanic clothes, giving Raven's mom a quick kiss before rushing out the door. The morning hustle and bustle filled the air with energy, but Raven's mind was already wandering to the adventure awaiting her outside.

"Hey mom, I've got something I want to do before school today," Raven said, as she finished the last bite of her cereal.

"Yeah, what's that?" Her mom replied, turning to face Raven with a questioning smile on her face.

"I want to go practice my net throwing on the beach," Raven replied, knowing full well that her mom wouldn't believe her about a talking tree.

"Well, have fun then," her mom said, turning back around, "I'm glad you're getting to spend some time outside before going to school all day."

Raven smiled, her excitement bubbling as she dashed upstairs to grab her backpack and the paper with the foggy designs she had drawn. In no time, she was back downstairs and out the door, planting quick kisses on her little siblings Kai and Naya's foreheads as she hurried past them. Making some black tailed deer prance away in fear with her vigor, she ran to the south side of the house, where her window was. Slowly, she brought up the piece of paper, twisting it until the lines faced from the earth to the sky. Back and forth she looked, from the drawn path to the trees. Raven sighed. She saw no similarities. So instead of following her make-shift map, she just started walking south. Raven passed the grass in her yard, and went into the small forest area beyond. There were salmonberries and alder trees, but those plants covered the entire island, so she didn't think much of it. Raven gazed through the trees, trying to find a slope downwards. Then she remembered, the tree was on a viewpoint, by the water! She had been so busy with the map and the cedar tree that she had completely forgotten the view. Pleased with herself, she smiled. Raven knew exactly how to get to the water. She ran back to their bright red house, grabbed her bike from the garage, and started her way to the south side of the island.

Her legs moved swiftly, past the Westside Highway stables onto Wax Orchard Road. She passed the Christensen Pond Preserve and Wilbie Farm, waving a hello to the goats on her way. As she pedaled along the familiar roads, Raven felt a sense of calm wash over her. She loved exploring the island, and knew it like the back of her hand. She had been biking these roads for years, and had always found solace in the quiet countryside. The stables and farms she passed were a reminder that people here still had a strong connection to the land and the animals that lived on it. Suddenly, the wind started to pick up. Raven's calm was interrupted by a jolt of cold air. She felt fear, and excitement. She could feel a strange energy coursing through her body, making her heart race with anticipation. The red rock in her pocket grew warmer with every passing moment, and she knew that something was about to happen.

As Raven pedaled down the winding road, the wind seemed to whisper secrets in her ears, urging her to venture further. It swirled around her, pushing her bike to the right, down a narrow path she hadn't noticed before. Despite her initial surprise, Raven felt a surge of excitement building within her. With each gust of wind, she felt a sense of freedom and exhilaration, as if the very elements themselves were guiding her towards her destiny.

As the road sloped downward, Raven's bike picked up speed, propelling her forward with increasing velocity. The wind grew stronger, whipping around her with greater force, tangling her hair and causing her clothes to flutter wildly in the breeze. Yet, amidst the chaos of the rushing wind, Raven remained steadfast, her eyes focused on the path ahead. As she approached the trailhead at the bottom of the hill, Raven's heart raced with anticipation. She braced herself as she skidded her bike to the left, kicking up wet mud at the base of the trail to avoid careening into the dense woods. With a quick glance at the red rock nestled securely in her pocket, Raven whispered words of encouragement to herself.

"Come on, rock," she murmured, her voice filled with excitement and determination. "You've gotta keep me alive."

With a surge of adrenaline, Raven kicked her legs over the frame of her bike and dismounted, feeling the soft soil yield beneath her feet as she gently laid the bike down. Standing there, with her heart pounding and her breath coming in quick bursts, Raven knew that the time had come to continue her journey on foot. Closing her eyes for a moment, Raven took a deep breath, the familiar warmth of the red rock comforting her as she prepared to step into the unknown. As she crossed the threshold into the forest, she felt a sense of reverence wash over her. The air was alive with the sounds of nature—the gentle rustle of leaves, the distant cry of a raven echoing through the trees. Her father's stories echoed in her mind, reminding her of the significance of the raven in their culture. According to him, the raven was revered as a trickster, a powerful being capable of transformation and change. He spoke of its ability to bring clarity to visions and guide those who sought its wisdom. Raven couldn't help but feel a sense of connection to her namesake as she heard the raven's call. She had been named after the raven for a reason, her father had always said. It was a reminder of the strength and resilience that ran through her veins. She could feel the warmth of the rock pulsing in her pocket, a steady guide leading her down the path ahead. As her eyes fluttered open again, she saw the deep green leaves on evergreen trees, and the bright color of the new spring saplings. Raven smelled the crisp air filled with the remnants of rain. Digging her hand into the moss growing out of a vine maple, she pulled out the root of a licorice fern. Cleaning it, she put it in her mouth and sucked on it as if it was nature's hard candy.

She followed the path, up a small hill, and then down a large slope. Just like in her dream, the evergreen trees swayed, and the salmonberry snagged at her clothes. Raven felt a deep sense of nervousness as she steadied herself on the alder and vine maple. As she continued down the trail, the dense foliage of the forest started to envelop her, blocking out most of the sunlight. What was once a bright and sunny day was now replaced by a dim, filtered light that cast an eerie, otherworldly glow. The shadows danced and flickered around her, causing her to feel uneasy and on edge. The wind whispered, cold in her ears. As she tried to keep her balance on the sloping ground, she suddenly slipped on a patch of mud, her feet flying out from under her. She landed hard on her back, feeling the wet earth seeping through her clothes and covering her school backpack in mud. She groaned in frustration, feeling disheartened.

As she lay there, her mind began to wander, and her initial determination began to falter. Doubt crept into her thoughts, and she started to worry about the consequences of her adventure. Her family and school obligations started to weigh heavily on her mind. The thought of her teacher calling her parents if she didn't show up on time made her heart race. She couldn't risk getting in trouble. She sighed, and stood up, reaching for a nearby sword fern frond to wipe off the mud from her clothes and backpack. At this point, the mud had caked on and wouldn't easily come off. As she wiped, she groaned in frustration as the mud seemed to just stick more to her clothes. She looked back up the hill she had just climbed down. It looked steep and treacherous, and she wondered if it was even worth continuing. As the doubt grew stronger, she thought about abandoning her adventure altogether and heading back home. The idea of playing her Nintendo Switch instead seemed much more appealing than slogging through the forest, especially if this was just some elaborate dream. But then she remembered the warmth of the rock in her pocket and the strange wind pushing her to this trail, it felt all too real to be a dream. She sighed again, giving up on removing the mud from her clothes, and turned back towards the downslope of the trail.

As she walked, the thick forest seemed endless, the towering trees seeming to go on forever, their branches creating a canopy that blocked out the sun. The trees seemed to twist and turn, the path never seeming to end. Just as she was beginning to really believe that there was no cedar tree and viewpoint at the end, the trees started to thin out and the light grew brighter. The rays of the sun shone through the leaves, casting dancing shadows on the forest floor. She quickened her pace, her heart pounding with excitement and relief as she stepped out of the dense foliage and into the warmth of the sun.

The air was cool and crisp, and the scent of pine and cedar filled her nostrils. As she stepped closer, her eyes widened at the sight of the massive cedar tree. *It's real,* she thought in awe, *the dream was real.* The cedar's branches reached high towards the sky as it swayed gently in the breeze, its leaves rustling as if it was whispering secrets to the wind. The tree's bark was rough and textured, with deep grooves and knots that gave it character and depth. As Raven stood in awe of the tree, she felt a sense of deep reverence. Beyond the cedar tree, the landscape stretched out before her, a patchwork of greens and browns. Rolling hills and forests extended into the distance, their colors blending and shifting in the light. The sky above was a deep blue, dotted with fluffy white clouds that floated lazily by. Raven took a deep breath, letting the beauty of the scene wash over her. In this moment, she felt some of the nervousness and fear melt away.

Despite the beauty and awe-inspiring nature of the scene before her, Raven couldn't help but feel a prickling sense of skepticism climb up her back. She had heard stories of mystical journeys and enchanted forests. In fact, she'd always wanted to live in the Pokemon world with all the epic creatures and magical places. But just like the stories her mother had told her of her ancestors, she had always dismissed all of them as fairy tales. Yet, here she was, standing before a massive cedar tree that a dream had led her to, with a seemingly magical red rock in her pocket. While part of her wanted to believe that this place was real, another part of her couldn't shake the feeling that it was all just a trick of the mind, an illusion created by her own imagination. Pinching herself, Raven attempted to jolt herself awake from what could only be a dream.

"Ouch," she murmured, observing the pink skin where she had pinched herself, before shifting her gaze back to the stunning tree before her. Despite the mesmerizing sight, she couldn't help but ponder whether there was a logical explanation for all of this or if it was an experience beyond her understanding.

As Raven reached into her pocket, the red rock warmed beneath her touch, pulsing with an otherworldly energy. With a sense of anticipation, she pulled it out, and in that moment, a sudden gust of wind tore through the forest, swirling around the massive cedar tree as if it had been waiting for this precise moment to unleash its power. The branches of the cedar tree thrashed wildly in the wind, casting eerie shadows that danced across Raven's face. Her hair whipped around her like a tempest as she clutched the rock tightly, her heart pounding with a potent mix of excitement and fear. But amidst the chaos of the wind, something incredible began to happen. As Raven held the rock, she felt a strange sensation wash over her—a whispering in the wind, soft and insistent, like the murmurs of her tribal ancestors speaking to her from beyond the veil of time. And as she listened, her senses were flooded with vivid visions of her people, their faces etched with determination and pride, their voices echoing in her mind. Raven felt a surge of emotions welling up inside her—a deep connection to her roots, a profound sense of belonging. In that moment, as she gazed out at the stunning vista before her, her senses heightened by the magic of the rock, she knew with absolute certainty that she was not alone. She was surrounded by the spirits of her ancestors, guiding her on her journey with their wisdom and strength. But as suddenly as it had begun, the wind died down and the visions faded away, leaving Raven standing alone in the quiet of the forest. Raven had released the rock, her hand shaking with excitement. She knew in that moment that the rock was something special, a powerful connection to her people and their legacy. Raven sensed an undeniable connection between the tree and the rock, a bond that went beyond the wind's playful movements in the branches. She remembered her mother telling her stories of the tribe emerging from the red clay, not dissimilar to the rock she held in her hand. It was as if the tree and the rock were intertwined, two parts of a greater whole that she couldn't comprehend.

As Raven approached the base of the cedar tree, she pulled the magical red rock from her pocket, feeling its weight and warmth in her palm. As she took a deep breath to slow her heart, she felt a sense of purpose and reverence wash over her. She carefully placed it on the largest root of the tree. The wind started to rise in response. This time, just a slow breeze that tickled her cheeks. Feeling the purpose inside, she knew what to do next. She began to collect cedar branches and leaves from the ground, laying them in a circle around the rock. As she worked, she felt a deep sense of respect for the cedar tree, knowing somehow that it had been in relationship for generations with her tribal ancestors in their ceremonies and rituals.

With the cedar circle in place, Raven turned her attention to marking the four directions. She carefully plucked moss and lichen from the earth, placing it at each point on the circle to create a symbolic representation of the earth, air, fire, and water. Finally, Raven took a cedar cone and placed it on top of the rock, creating an altar for her ceremony. As she stepped back and admired her work, she felt a profound sense of connection to the land and her ancestors wash over her in a way she had never experienced before. It was as if the spirits of her indigenous ancestors had guided her hands, helping her remember how to be in connection with the earth, how to hold a ceremony. In that moment, she felt an overwhelming sense of belonging and connection to the land and her ancestors, as if all the stories and traditions she had inherited were pulsating through her veins. It felt uncanny and strange to feel so certain of herself and her heritage. It was as if the act of creating this simple yet powerful symbol had unlocked a hidden part of herself, a part that had been waiting to be discovered amidst the quiet whispers of the trees and the ancient stones that surrounded her.

With her legs crossed and her eyes fixed on the towering cedar tree above, Raven settled at the base of the altar she had crafted. Though a sense of conviction had coursed through her veins just moments before, she now felt that certainty begin to ebb away.

"Well, this is it," she mused to herself, feeling a tinge of doubt creeping in. "Maybe I should give it a try and see if this tree can actually talk."

Raven leaned in, focusing her attention on the rustling leaves and the creaking branches, hoping for a sign, a whisper, or any sort of response from the ancient giant that loomed above her, she looked around, to make sure no one was there; she didn't want to be seen talking to the cedar if it didn't reply. She took a deep breath, feeling the cool forest air fill her lungs, and spoke quietly to the tree.

"Cedar tree," she said, her voice barely above a whisper. "You spoke to me in my dream. I wonder what you have to say to me now?"

As she waited for a response, Raven felt a sense of nervousness wash over her. Listening intently, she heard the sound of the wind rustling through the branches of the cedar tree, but no voices. She listened harder, but heard nothing. Slumping her shoulders, she started to think it was all just a ruse; something her mind made up. She looked down at her little nature altar, and scuffed the dirt around it, feeling silly about how excited she had been. Suddenly, she heard a voice in her mind, a deep and ancient voice that seemed to come from the very heart of the cedar tree itself.

"Raven," the voice said, startling her. "You are a child of the earth, a keeper of the land. You have been raised without the stories of our ancestors. I'll share those with you in trust that you will hold them and share them with love."

Raven's heart skipped a beat as the voice echoed in her ears. She felt a shiver run down her spine, and her breath caught in her throat. This was real, and it was scary. The world around her seemed to blur, and all she could focus on was the weight of the words that had just been spoken. She had always felt a deep connection to the land, but this was different. This was something sacred, something that she had never experienced before.

"Holy moly," she breathed. Those were the only words she could manage. Raven sat there in stunned silence, feeling the full weight of what had just happened. She looked around her, taking in the majesty of the cedar tree and the beauty of the forest that surrounded her. It was all so different from the world of Pokémon adventures that she had grown up reading about. This was real life, and it felt overwhelming.

Raven looked up at the cedar tree towering above her, feeling small and insignificant in its shadow. She had always felt a deep connection to nature, but now that she had received a response, it was almost too much to bear.

"This is real," she whispered to herself, feeling a surge of fear and excitement coursing through her veins. She took a deep breath, trying to steady her nerves. Her hands shook as she clasped them tightly in her lap, and she could feel a knot of nervousness forming in her stomach. The responsibility of being a keeper of the land weighed heavily upon her, and she knew that she had a lot to learn.

"Holy moly," she breathed, her voice barely above a whisper. "This is really happening." She looked down, steadying her voice.

"I'll do my best," she whispered, feeling a sense of determination rising within her. Raven knew that the road ahead would not be easy, but she was ready to embrace the challenge.

The cedar tree rustled as if it was preparing to tell a story deep from the earth. "Before the ones with white skin and blue eyes arrived," the tree began, "your people lived in harmony with the land and the sea. They had a deep understanding of the cycles of nature, and life was built around the changing seasons and the bountiful resources of this island."

As the cedar spoke, Raven listened with rapt attention, her nerves still jangling with the weight of the tree's earlier words. The tree's voice was deep and resounding, like the rumble of thunder in the distance.

"Under my branches," the tree's voice murmured softly, carrying with it the weight of centuries past, "there was a great feast every year to honor the salmon, a celebration that echoed through the ages like a timeless melody. The fishers of our tribe would venture out into the waters, their hands deftly wielding nets and hooks, their spirits attuned to the rhythm of the river. With each catch, they would offer thanks to the spirits of the salmon, recognizing the sacred bond between our people and these noble creatures of the water.

"It was during one of these feasts that a tale was told—a tale that would become woven into the fabric of our tribe for generations to come. It was the story of a young boy, a boy who wandered the streams near our village with a heart full of curiosity and wonder, not unlike you Raven. One day, as he cast his gaze upon the shimmering waters, he spotted a small salmon, its scales glinting in the sunlight. Moved by the fish's beauty and grace, and by his hunger, the boy reached out and gently captured it in his hands.

But as he held the salmon in his grasp, something remarkable happened. The fish, instead of struggling against him, looked up with eyes that seemed to hold the wisdom of the ages. In that moment, the boy felt a connection unlike any he had ever known—a connection that transcended the boundaries of species and spoke to the very essence of his being.

With a heart full of compassion, the boy made a decision—a decision that would forever alter the course of his life and the destiny of our tribe. He set the salmon free, watching as it darted back into the embrace of the river, its spirit unbroken and its gratitude palpable in the air.

And then, to the boy's astonishment, the salmon spoke—a voice as clear and melodious as the waters themselves. It thanked him for his kindness and promised to return in a few months' time, accompanied by others of its kind, to share in the abundance of the river with our people.

True to its word, when the seasons turned and the salmon began their journey upstream once more, they returned to our village in a grand procession, their silver scales gleaming in the sunlight as they leapt joyfully through the waters. Our people welcomed them with open arms, honoring them as sacred beings and treating them with the utmost respect and reverence.

And so it was that the bond between our tribe and the salmon grew stronger with each passing year, a testament to the power of compassion, gratitude, and the enduring spirit of the natural world."

Raven couldn't help but feel a sense of awe at the story, but it also made her feel sad. She had grown up in a world where salmon came from the grocery store, not from the sea, and the idea of catching a fish with her bare hands seemed like something out of a fairy tale. She wondered what it would have been like to live in a world where the land and sea were so intertwined, where life was connected and sacred. As the cedar fell silent, Raven sat there for a moment, lost in thought. She felt grateful for the tree's words, but also a little overwhelmed. She had so much to learn, and the weight of her responsibility as a keeper of the stories felt heavier than ever before.

Raven snapped out of her trance as the tree's voice trailed off, and a wave of doubt washed over her. Did she really just hear the tree talk, or was it all just in her head? She shook her head, trying to dispel the disbelief, but it lingered like a persistent fog.

Raven stood up slowly, still feeling a bit woozy from the experience. As she approached the cedar tree, Raven felt a mixture of curiosity and apprehension. She examined the tree's bark and branches, searching for any sign of where the voice might have come from. But the more she looked, the more she realized how impossible it was for a tree to speak. Despite her rational mind telling her it wasn't possible, Raven had heard the tree's voice with her own ears. Her heart raced with both excitement and fear as she circled the tree, trying to make sense of what had just happened. It was a feeling unlike any other, a mix of wonder and uncertainty that left her on edge. This was not normal. Trees don't talk. People don't hear voices from nature.

But at the same time, Raven couldn't deny the feeling of connection and understanding that flowed between her and the cedar. She shook her head and took a deep breath, trying to steady herself. Maybe it was just her imagination playing tricks on her. But as she looked back at the cedar, she saw its branches rustling again, and the voice resumed.

"There is also the story of the thunderbird," it said in a hushed voice. As the cedar spoke, its words seemed to resonate with a truth that transcended mere storytelling, stirring something deep within Raven's soul. She felt a shiver of anticipation ripple through her as she listened, her senses alive with the magic of the moment. It was as if the very air around her crackled with energy, charged with the power of the thunderbird's legend.

"The thunderbird," the cedar began, its voice a gentle melody that seemed to echo through the forest, "was not merely a creature of myth and legend, but a guardian of the skies, a protector of all who dwelled beneath its watchful gaze."

Raven's heart quickened with each word, her imagination soaring on the wings of the thunderbird's tale. She could almost see the majestic creature, its wings spread wide against the backdrop of the stormy sky, its eyes flashing with the brilliance of lightning.

"Described as a supernatural being," the cedar continued, its branches swaying in time with the rhythm of its words, "the thunderbird embodied the very essence of power and strength. With each beat of its mighty wings, it stirred the wind to life, sending ripples of thunder echoing through the heavens."

As Raven listened, she felt a sense of wonder wash over her—a reverence for the thunderbird and all that it represented. It was more than just a story—it was a testament to the resilience of the human spirit, a reminder of the enduring bond between nature and humanity.

"The thunderbird was revered by our people as a protector," the cedar went on, its voice soft yet filled with a deep sense of reverence. "A guardian of the skies, a beacon of hope in times of darkness and despair."

Raven's eyes widened with wonder as the cedar tree wove the story of the thunderbird. She felt a sense of awe and reverence for the powerful bird and the traditions of her ancestors. The cedar's voice was soothing and reassuring, and Raven found herself relaxing into the experience, forgetting her initial fear and disbelief. She realized that she was experiencing something profound and magical, and she didn't want it to end.

As the cedar finished recounting the stories of her people, the wind seemed to quieten, and Raven looked up with a longing gaze.

"Please, one more story?" she pleaded.

The cedar, sensing her desire for more, obliged and continued to weave the tales of the past. "One of the most revered creatures is the orca," it said with reverence. "Legends tell of a human who was transformed into this powerful sea creature to protect and guide the tribal people. The orca is a sacred animal that holds the power to communicate with us through dreams and visions, a guardian and guide that we respect and honor."

In a voice that seemed to carry the weight of centuries, the cedar tree began to weave its tale, its words weaving a tapestry of wonder and magic that enveloped Raven in its embrace.

"Long ago," the cedar began, its voice a gentle whisper that danced on the wind, "a young indigenous man set out to sea in search of food for his family. His canoe sliced through the waters, his heart filled with hope and determination. But as the days passed and the sun sank below the horizon, his nets remained empty, his efforts thwarted by the elusive fish that danced just out of reach."

Raven's breath caught in her throat as she listened, her imagination conjuring images of the young man's solitary journey across the vast expanse of the ocean. She could feel the weight of his disappointment, the ache of his longing for home.

"And then," the cedar continued, its branches swaying gently in the breeze, "as he prepared to turn back, a storm swept in from the horizon, its fury unleashed upon the sea. The young man's canoe was tossed and turned by the raging waves, his heart pounding in his chest as he fought to keep his balance."

As the cedar spoke, Raven could almost taste the salt spray on her lips, feel the sting of the wind against her cheeks. She leaned in closer, her senses alive with the energy of the moment.

"But just when it seemed that all hope was lost," the cedar went on, its voice tinged with awe, "a pod of orca appeared, their sleek black bodies slicing through the water like knives. They encircled the young man's canoe, their presence a beacon of hope in the midst of the storm."

"Filled with gratitude for their protection," the cedar continued, its voice soft yet filled with reverence, "the young man decided to honor the orca by creating a totem pole in their likeness. With each stroke of his chisel, he poured his heart and soul into the wood, his dreams infused with the spirit of the sea."

As the cedar spoke, Raven felt a shiver of anticipation ripple through her, her heart pounding in her chest. She could sense the magic of the moment, the power of the young man's vision.

"And then," the cedar concluded, its voice a gentle murmur that seemed to fade into the twilight, "in his dreams, the orca came to him, their words a whisper on the wind. They told him of their origins, of their transformation from human to sea creature, and of their sacred duty to protect and guide the tribal people."

Raven listened with wonder to the cedar's tale, feeling a deeper connection to the island and the creatures that had long inhabited it. The sky was starting to darken, and the wind started to pick up. The day had passed so quickly, and it was almost night.

"Thank you, Cedar," Raven expressed with utmost gratitude. "I need to go home before my parents worry. Can I come back tomorrow to hear more?"

With the cedar's tale still echoing in her mind, Raven felt a surge of anticipation coursing through her veins. As she delicately retrieved the red rock from the altar, its smooth surface warming beneath her touch, she knew that her journey was far from over. With a sense of purpose burning bright within her, she turned to leave the shelter of the ancient cedar, her heart pounding with excitement.

As Raven made her way back up the hill, the forest seemed to close in around her, the once-familiar path now obscured by looming shadows and tangled undergrowth. With each step, the air grew thick with a sense of foreboding, and Raven couldn't shake the feeling that she was being watched.

Just as she was about to quicken her pace, a haunting howl pierced the stillness of the forest, sending a chill down her spine. Raven's heart skipped a beat as she strained to locate the source of the sound, her senses on high alert. Was it the cry of a lone wolf, or something else entirely? For a moment, Raven stood frozen in place, her breath catching in her throat as she listened intently. Then, without warning, the howl echoed once more, closer this time, and accompanied by a chorus of eerie caws from the surrounding trees. It was as if the very forest itself had come alive with the sound of predators on the prowl.

With her heart pounding in her chest, Raven knew that she had to keep moving, to push through the fear that threatened to paralyze her. Gripping the red rock tightly in her hand, she took a deep breath and forged ahead, her footsteps quick and determined as she navigated the treacherous terrain.

But as she pressed on, the night air became still and quiet, echoing through the darkness like a haunting melody. Raven's pulse quickened with each passing moment, her mind racing with thoughts of what lurked in the shadows just beyond her sight. Suddenly, a flash of movement caught her eye—a sleek, black shape soaring through the moonlit sky. Raven's breath caught in her throat as she watched the majestic bird circle overhead, its sharp eyes fixed on her with a gaze that seemed to pierce through the darkness.

With a sense of relief flooding through her, Raven's heart swelled as she recognized the sleek, black shape soaring through the moonlit sky. It was a raven, her namesake, and in its presence, she felt a deep sense of connection and comfort. As the majestic bird circled overhead, its sharp eyes fixed on her with a gaze that seemed to pierce through the darkness, Raven couldn't help but feel a surge of gratitude wash over her. With newfound confidence coursing through her veins, Raven walked calmly up the rest of the hill, her steps steady and sure despite the lingering shadows that clung to the edges of the forest. The presence of the raven seemed to imbue her with a sense of strength and resilience, guiding her through the darkness and lighting her way with its silent vigil.

As she reached the crest of the hill, Raven turned to look back at the forest below, her gaze lingering on the spot where she had encountered the majestic bird. Though the night was still and quiet, she could feel the weight of its presence lingering in the air.

Raven pedaled home as the evening shadows stretched across the island, carrying the tales of the cedar tree with her. The scent of the sea lingered in the air as she approached her house, her thoughts consumed by the cedar's stories and the secrets shared between the ancient tree and herself.

Entering her home, she was greeted by the savory aroma of dinner wafting from the kitchen. Her mom, dad, and siblings were gathered around the table, their faces a mix of relief and curiosity as they saw her.

"Raven, where were you all day?" her mom asked, concern etched on her face.

"Yeah, we got a notification from the school saying you missed all of your classes," added her dad, his tone serious.

Raven's mind raced, torn between the truth and a different reality. The image of the cedar tree lingered in her thoughts, distracting her from the questions at hand. "Oh, uh, I was at school all day. Just lost track of time," she replied, her eyes avoiding direct contact.

Her siblings, Naya and Kai exchanged skeptical glances, but her mom sighed, "Raven, we worry about you. You can't just skip classes like that."

As they sat down for dinner, Raven's mind wandered between the cedar's tales and the facade she had just created. The delicious smells of the meal filled the air, but her thoughts were anchored to the stories of the orca and the sacred totem pole.

"So, what did you learn in school today?" her dad inquired, breaking through her reverie.

Raven hesitated for a moment before offering a vague response, "You know, the usual stuff. Math, English, and all that." Her mind, however, was far away, sailing on the sea of the cedar's wisdom.

Her mom studied her with a discerning gaze, sensing that something was amiss. "Are you sure everything's okay, Raven?"

Caught in the web of her own fabrication, Raven mustered a forced smile, "Yeah, Mom, everything's fine. Just had a lot on my mind."

They continued to eat their dinner. The warmth of the family gathered around the table contrasting with the internal conflict Raven grappled with. As she savored each bite, the cedar's stories echoed in her thoughts, intertwining with the fabric of her reality. Raven couldn't shake the feeling that her journey was only beginning, and the cedar's wisdom had set her on a course she couldn't easily navigate.

As dinner progressed, Raven couldn't silence the nagging curiosity within her. Unable to resist, she decided to probe her parents about some of the stories she had heard—stories that felt ancient yet remarkably alive in her mind.

"Hey, Mom, Dad," she began hesitantly, "have you ever heard the story of the orca guiding the indigenous man back to shore?"

Her parents exchanged a knowing glance, a flicker of recognition in their eyes. "Oh, that's a beautiful tale," her mom chimed in with a warm smile. "The orca is a sacred creature to our people. It's said to have once been a human, transformed by the Creator to protect and guide us."

Her dad nodded in agreement, "Yes, the story goes that the young man, in gratitude for the orca's help, carved a totem pole in its likeness. And in his dream, the orca revealed its human past and its mission to safeguard the tribal people."

Raven's eyes widened with excitement. "And what about the totem poles? Are there more stories about them?"

Her mom chuckled, "Absolutely, Raven. Totem poles are like storytellers themselves, preserving the history and legends of our people. Each carving has a unique tale to tell, connecting us to our ancestors and the land."

Her dad added, "Totem poles often depict animals like the orca, representing traits and values important to our community. They're a way of passing down our culture through generations."

Later that evening, Raven's dad quietly walked into her room, spotting her huddled under the covers, fully engrossed in her virtual adventures on the Nintendo Switch. The soft glow from the screen painted her face as she skillfully navigated her favorite games. Lost in the pixelated world, Raven hardly noticed her dad's gentle entrance until he reminded her, "Hey Raven, it's bedtime. Time to turn off the Switch and get some sleep."

A sense of reluctance washed over her, and a twinge of sadness shimmered in her eyes as she reluctantly powered down the console. It was like bidding farewell to a digital friend, and Raven couldn't help but feel a mix of emotions. The vibrant landscapes and exciting challenges now vanished, leaving the room in quiet darkness.

As Raven's dad settled on the edge of her bed, he reached over, brushing a loose strand of hair from her face. The room seemed to embrace them with warmth and love during this serene family moment. In that brief switch from the virtual to the real world, Raven experienced a yearning, a hint of melancholy as if she was leaving behind a piece of herself in the gaming universe.

"Dad, just one more second," Raven pleaded with a hopeful glint in her eyes, not ready to part ways with the captivating virtual realm. Her dad let out a soft chuckle, fully understanding her reluctance.

"Alright, one more second, my little gamer," he agreed, and Raven savored those precious extra moments, soaking in the final echoes of her digital adventure before surrendering to the world of dreams.

Reluctantly, she set aside her console and nestled under her cozy blanket. As he tucked the blanket around her, Raven's curiosity bubbled up. "Dad, can I ask you something?"

He nodded, a comforting smile on his face. "Of course, sweetheart. What's on your mind?"

Raven hesitated before posing her question. "What does being indigenous mean to you? Like, how do you feel about it?"

Her dad sighed, a thoughtful expression on his face. "Being indigenous means being connected to a rich history, to the land, and to a vibrant culture. It's a source of pride for us, Raven."

He added, "But it's not always easy, especially living here on Vashon Island. Most people around us are non-Native, and being recognized as indigenous can be challenging. We've faced moments where we felt like outsiders. It's tough when the culture of our people is so different from the majority. Sometimes, it feels like we have to present ourselves in a way that others expect to be seen and recognized."

He continued, "But, Raven, it's crucial to hold on to our roots, to the culture of the tribal people. Our struggle doesn't diminish the importance of keeping our traditions alive. We've been going through a bit of a challenge lately, trying to find that balance."

Raven listened intently, absorbing his words. "I understand. Thank you for sharing that with me."

Raven's dad sat down on the edge of her bed, his face carrying a weight of history and a determination to pass on the truth. Raven, looking up at her father with wide eyes, sensed the gravity of his words.

"Dreamer, I need you to know something important," he began, his voice steady. "Our journey as indigenous people has been filled with struggle and resilience. Back in the 1880s, Native parents, just like your great-grandparents, were forced to send their children to boarding schools."

He paused, allowing the weight of history to settle in the room. "These were not places of learning and growth. Instead, they were places where our culture was intentionally destroyed, and abuse was rampant. Imagine being a child, taken away from your family, your traditions, and forced to conform to a foreign way of life."

Her dad's eyes glistened with a mixture of sorrow and determination as he continued, "In 1893, settlers even burned Herring's House, the last Duwamish longhouse on the estuary of the river for whom they were named."

He took a deep breath, trying to find the right words to convey the pain endured by his ancestors. "Your grandmother, my mom, tried to escape one of these schools with her best friend. Unfortunately, they got caught. The punishments were cruel—tied up, hands behind their backs, left in the hallway. If they fell or slept, the matron would hear, and they'd be whipped, forced to stand again."

Her dad's gaze turned to the window, as if searching for solace in the night sky. "Our culture was systematically smashed and robbed from us inside those death camps they called boarding schools. The destruction of elders and matriarchs left a void, a disconnect from the ancient wisdom that once surrounded us."

He reached out, gently placing a hand on Raven's shoulder, his touch filled with both pain and hope. "Before contact with the white folks, elders would surround us inside our longhouse, imparting wisdom from the first breath until it became an inseparable part of who we are. Now, we've become rich people in a different way."

Her dad's eyes met Raven's, his voice unwavering. "I want you to be rich, Dreamer, in the teachings of Mother Earth, in the water, in the circle of life. Our journey is one of reclaiming what was stolen, of resilience, and of passing on the wisdom that survived despite the attempts to erase it."

"Our connection to water is more than just a way of life; it's the heartbeat of our people. For generations, we've lived along these waterways, our ancestors gliding in dugout canoes crafted from the sturdy cedar trees that surround us. The ocean and rivers weren't just pathways; they were our lifeblood, providing not just food but also the routes for trade that connected tribes across the land.

Here on Vashon Island, where the forests meet the water, we learn from the land itself. Each tree, each rock, each wave carries stories from those who walked these shores before us. It's like a living classroom, teaching us about our heritage and the natural world that sustains us.

And fishing, Dreamer, it's not just a skill; it's a connection to our ancestors. When we cast our nets and catch salmon, it's like reaching back through time, honoring the traditions passed down through generations. It's our way of holding hands with those who came before us.

I want you to know, even though we've faced challenges and heartache, we haven't given up. We're resilient, just like the cedar trees standing tall in our forests. We've adapted, finding new ways to keep our heritage alive. The connection we have to the water, the forests, and the traditions of our ancestors is what makes us strong. It might look different now, but the essence of who we are and where we come from remains deeply rooted in the land and water that surround us on Vashon Island."

Raven's eyes sparkled with a mix of excitement and understanding. "Wow, Dad, that's amazing! So, like, the island is our history book, and the water and trees are the stories? And when we fish, it's like having a chat with our ancestors? That's pretty cool. I guess I never really thought about it that way."

She grinned, the gears turning in her young mind. "And, yeah, I know we've faced some tough stuff, but we're still here, right? Like, we didn't give up. I want to learn more, Dad. Can you teach me all the cool stuff about our island and our people? And maybe, just maybe, we can have our own epic fishing adventure, the way our ancestors did!"

Raven's dad chuckled warmly, his eyes reflecting a mix of pride and love. "Maybe, kiddo. Maybe." He ruffled her hair gently and stood up. "Now, it's time for dreams and adventures. Close your eyes, Dreamer."

He moved to the doorway, turning off the light, leaving only the soft glow of the moon filtering through the curtains. "Sleep well, and dream of the stories the island has to tell."

With that, he left Raven's room, the door closing gently behind him. In the quiet darkness, Raven snuggled under her covers, the whispers of the island echoing in her mind. She closed her eyes, ready to embark on dreams filled with the tales of the water, the trees, and the adventures yet to come.

That night, Raven nestled the rock beneath her pillow, her mind buzzing with excitement and anticipation. She couldn't wait to see what adventures awaited her in the realm of dreams, especially after the magical experience she had with the cedar tree earlier. With a contented sigh, she closed her eyes and let sleep carry her away.

In her dream, Raven found herself standing on the shore of the ocean, the moon casting a silver glow on the dark waves. The air was cool and crisp, filled with the salty tang of the sea. As she gazed out at the vast expanse of water before her, Raven felt a sense of peace wash over her—a deep connection to the rhythm of the tides and the timeless beauty of the ocean. Suddenly, a majestic orca breached the surface of the water, its sleek body glistening in the moonlight. Raven's heart skipped a beat as she watched in awe, her eyes locked on the magnificent creature as it swam gracefully through the waves. With each powerful stroke of its tail, the orca propelled itself closer to the shore, its presence commanding respect and admiration. As the orca drew nearer, Raven could feel the rush of cool ocean breeze against her skin, the rhythmic sound of the waves crashing against the shore filling her ears. She held her breath, captivated by the beauty and grace of the creature before her. And then, with a gentle flick of its tail, the orca came to a stop just a few feet away from Raven, its dark eyes meeting hers with an intelligence that seemed to transcend words.

With a mix of excitement and apprehension coursing through her veins, Raven took a deep breath and climbed onto the orca's back. The sensation was unlike anything she had ever experienced before—exhilarating and thrilling, like riding the world's biggest roller coaster. As the orca started to glide through the water, Raven felt herself being carried away on a journey beyond her wildest dreams. The wind whipped through her hair, tangling it into a wild mess, while the rhythmic rise and fall of the orca beneath her sent shivers of excitement coursing through her body. With each powerful stroke of its tail, the orca propelled itself forward, slicing through the waves with effortless grace. Raven clung tightly to its sleek, muscular form, her heart pounding in her chest as she surrendered herself to the thrill of the ride. As they raced through the ocean, Raven felt a sense of freedom wash over her—a feeling of being untethered from the worries and cares of the world below. For in that moment, there was only her and the orca.

Taking a deep breath, Raven felt the cool spray of the ocean on her face as the orca dove beneath the surface. With a sense of anticipation coursing through her veins, she closed her eyes and surrendered herself to the unknown. As the world transformed around her, Raven found herself immersed in a magical underwater realm—a kaleidoscope of colors and shapes that danced before her eyes. Vibrant coral reefs stretched out in all directions, teeming with life as colorful fish darted and swirled through the crystal-clear waters. Raven marveled at the beauty that surrounded her, her heart swelling with wonder and awe. She felt weightless and free, suspended in the embrace of the ocean's depths, as if she had been transported to another world entirely.

As the orca breached the surface, Raven's ears popped with the change in pressure, a sensation that momentarily disoriented her. Then, in an instant, the thunderbird appeared above her, its massive wings outstretched and gleaming in the sunlight. With a graceful swoop, it gently lifted Raven from the orca's back, cradling her in its powerful talons as they soared into the vast expanse of the sky. The world below became a blur as they ascended higher and higher, leaving behind the shimmering surface of the ocean and entering a realm of boundless possibility. Raven felt a mix of awe and exhilaration wash over her, her heart racing with the thrill of being carried by such a magnificent creature. The thunderbird's booming voice echoed in her ears, reassuring her that she was safe in its grasp, and she couldn't help but marvel at the strength and grace of her airborne companion. As they soared through the endless expanse of the sky, Raven's senses were overwhelmed by the sights and sounds that surrounded her. The sky stretched out before her, a vast canvas of ever-changing colors and patterns, while the wind roared in her ears, whipping her hair into a frenzy. She could feel the feathers of the thunderbird brushing against her face, each touch a reminder of the cedar tree's story.

With a graceful descent, the thunderbird brought Raven to the edge of a rushing river. The air was filled with the sound of splashing water as salmon leaped upstream. Raven felt the cool mist on her face and the energy of the river flowing beneath her feet. She crouched down, and the salmon jumped over her, their sleek bodies shimmering in the moonlight.

As the first rays of sunlight painted Raven's room with a soft glow, she slowly opened her eyes, greeted by the familiar sight of her Pokémon poster hanging on the wall. A smile tugged at the corners of her lips as she lay there, basking in the lingering magic of her dream. But reality soon intruded on her reverie—it was Wednesday, a school day, and she could already hear the faint sound of her alarm clock ringing from across the room.

With a weary sigh, Raven sat up in bed, gently rubbing away the last traces of sleep from her eyes. As she glanced at her reflection in the dresser mirror, a curious glint sparkled in her eyes, and a faint smile played at the corners of her lips. The memories of her dream—the majestic orca, the soaring thunderbird, and the vibrant salmon—lingered vividly in her mind, refusing to fade with the morning light. Reality began to settle in as Raven reached for her phone, the familiar weight of responsibility pressing down on her shoulders. With a quick swipe, she scrolled through her messages, each notification a reminder of the impending transition from the whimsical realm of dreamland to the structured routine of school. Wednesday meant more than just the midweek mark—it was a day filled with classes, assignments, and the predictable rhythm of the school routine that awaited her. With a resigned nod to the inevitable, Raven pushed aside her lingering thoughts of adventure and reluctantly prepared herself to face the challenges of the day ahead.

With a mixture of reluctance and acceptance, Raven reached for her laptop and opened her web browser. Typing in "tribal people," she embarked on her quest for knowledge, her curiosity piqued by the remnants of her dream still lingering in her mind. As she hit the search button, a wave of anticipation washed over her, eager to uncover the mysteries of the indigenous cultures that had captivated her imagination.

The search results appeared on the screen, offering brief glimpses into the world of tribal people. Raven's eyes scanned the snippets of information, each one teasing her curiosity further. She read about the indigenous people of the water, who had thrived along the coastlines of the Pacific Northwest, harnessing the resources of the ocean to sustain their way of life. As Raven delved deeper into her search, she soon realized that the surface-level information provided only scratched the surface of these rich and complex cultures. Despite her efforts, the search yielded little more than a handful of scattered details, leaving her thirsting for a deeper understanding of her ancestors who called this land their home.

As Raven got ready for school, a mix of excitement and curiosity bubbled inside her like a pot of simmering anticipation. The magical stories from the cedar tree were still fresh in her mind, their lingering echoes urging her to seek out more of the ancient tree's wisdom.

Balancing the usual school routine with her yearning for the cedar's teachings, Raven formulated a plan. With a quick glance at the clock, she calculated that she could steal a few precious moments before the school day began. The idea of connecting with the wise cedar filled her with a sense of purpose and possibility, adding an extra sprinkle of magic to her otherwise ordinary morning. As she gathered her belongings, Raven couldn't help but feel a sense of excitement building within her, eager to see what secrets the cedar had yet to reveal.

In her rush down the stairs, Raven's backpack already slung over her shoulders, she spotted a box of Lucky Charms on the kitchen counter. Without a second thought, she poured a handful into her jacket pockets. Unable to resist, she tilted her head back and crunched on the cereal, letting the remaining charms tumble to the floor.

Darting towards the front door, she grabbed the matches from the windowsill next to the candles and slipped them into her pocket. A few cereal pieces beneath her feet caused a brief slip, but she recovered quickly, determined to reach the cedar tree. As she made her exit, her mom's voice rang out, reminding her to promise that she'd go to school. With a hasty acknowledgment, Raven called back, "I promise, Mom!" She hopped on her bike and pedaled away, leaving a frustrated little sister Naya behind, glaring at the empty Lucky Charms box.

The morning air enveloped Raven in its crisp embrace as she pedaled her way to the cedar tree, her anticipation growing with each turn of the pedals. The thought of hearing more stories from the wise ancestor tree filled her with a sense of eager anticipation, propelling her forward with renewed energy. As she rode, Raven reached into her pocket and pulled out a handful of Lucky Charms, the sugary sweetness of the cereal providing a comforting distraction as she journeyed deeper into the forest. With each bite, she savored the familiar taste, a small indulgence amidst the excitement of the morning.

Arriving at her destination, Raven leaned her bike against the sturdy trunk of an alder tree, its leaves rustling softly in the breeze. With a quickened pace, she made her way down the familiar trail, the earthy scent of the forest mingling with the sweet aroma of the cereal on her breath. Approaching the cedar tree, Raven felt a sense of calm wash over her, like a warm embrace from an old friend.

With a reverent touch, she retrieved the red rock from her pocket, feeling its weightiness in the palm of her hand. As she placed it back down on the altar, the breeze picked up around her, carrying with it the whispers of the forest and the ancient wisdom of the cedar tree.

"Good morning, Raven," said the cedar. "It's good to see you again."

"Good morning, Cedar," replied Raven. "I had the most amazing dream last night. I dreamed of the orca, the thunderbird, and the salmon."

The cedar had a smile in its voice as it spoke, "Those are powerful animals, Raven. What did you see in your dream?"

"I saw them swimming in the ocean, soaring through the sky, and leaping upstream," said Raven. "It was like they were all connected, all part of the same story."

The cedar nodded. "That's because they are. The orca, thunderbird, and salmon are all part of the natural world, and they all have a role to play. They are all connected, just like we are all connected."

Raven felt a sense of wonder wash over her. She had never thought about the world in that way before, as a place where everything was connected, where everything had a purpose.

"I want to learn more about my people," said Raven. "I want to understand how everything fits together, how everything works, how my people are connected to all of it."

The cedar smiled again. "That's a good desire, Raven. And I'm here to help you. Let's start with the orca. Do you know anything about them?"

Raven shook her head. "Not really. I just know they're powerful animals."

The cedar tree said, "You're right, but orcas are special not just because they're strong. They're like friends, living in groups and talking to each other using special sounds like clicks and whistles. They are also incredibly intelligent, with a brain that is larger and more complex than a human's."

Raven listened, fascinated. She had never thought about animals having complex communication systems or advanced intelligence.

"And they're also incredibly important to the ocean ecosystem," continued the cedar. "They help to maintain a balance by keeping other animal populations in check."

Raven felt a sense of awe wash over her. The orca was so much more than just a powerful symbol. It was a complex, intelligent, and vital part of the natural world.

Raven nodded, feeling inspired. "Wow, that's just amazing. I want to learn everything I can about the tribal people and their connection to nature." She paused, thinking for a moment. "Do you know if there are any books or websites that I can read to learn more?"

The cedar spoke up, "While it's good to learn from books and the internet, remember that the best way to truly understand something is to experience it for yourself. Why don't you go out into nature and see what you can find? Observe the plants, animals, and the environment around you. You may discover things that no book or website could ever teach you."

Raven thought about this for a moment, realizing the truth in the cedar's words. "You're right, thanks."

The cedar had a smile in its voice again, "You're welcome, Raven. And remember, there's always more to learn. The world is full of wonders and mysteries."

"Today I need to speak to you about the hardship that your people persevered through," the cedar tree sighed, "it's not easy to talk about, but I need for you to know the true stories, and for you to understand the resilience of your people." The cedar tree spoke with a heavy heart as it shared these difficult stories with Raven. It knew that these were not easy truths to face.

"In the face of great adversity, your people persevered," spoke the cedar tree in a solemn tone.

"When those with white skin and blue eyes first arrived, they brought with them diseases that our people had never encountered before, causing many to fall ill and perish. They hid the diseases in blankets they gave as gifts, and we died with those sheets wrapped around us. The settlers also brought weapons, and once we were weak from the sickness and grief, they attacked. We had to defend ourselves and our homes from attacks. But perhaps the most difficult decision our ancestors had to make was when they signed the Medicine Creek Treaty in 1854."

The cedar tree paused, as if feeling the weight of the memory. "The tribal people had some understanding of the Medicine Creek Treaty when it was signed, but they did not fully comprehend the consequences of what they were agreeing to," explained the cedar tree. "The treaty was written in English, a language that most of our people did not speak or read, and it was also deliberately vague in certain areas. Some of the promises made in the treaty were not kept by the US government, and the tribal people were further mistreated in the years that followed. The treaty promised us a reservation, ability to fish and hunt in our traditional lands and some other benefits, but in exchange, we had to give up most of our land and be subject to the authority of the US government. It was a choice that came with great sacrifice and uncertainty, but our people held on to our culture and traditions nonetheless. The medicine women continued to use their healing powers to help our people, and the elders passed down stories and teachings to the younger generations."

Raven listened intently to the cedar's words, her eyes wide with curiosity and concern. As the cedar spoke of the hardships faced by her people, Raven's heart grew heavy with sadness. She couldn't imagine what it must have been like for her ancestors to go through such difficult times.

When the cedar finished speaking, Raven took a deep breath and looked up at the tree. "Thank you for telling me about this," she said, "I'm so grateful that you're here to continue teaching me the history of my people."

The breeze rustled the cedar's leaves. "That's enough for today, I need to rest so I may share more in the future," the tree murmured.

Its spirit seemed to turn to face the water. It seemed as if it had a longing to touch the sea. Raven took a deep breath, smelling the salty air and watching the beautiful clouds as they softly shimmered in the sky. Though she knew she had to go to school, Raven couldn't help but linger a little while longer, basking in the tranquility of the moment. Leaning against the trunk of the cedar tree, she closed her eyes and let herself be carried away by the gentle rhythm of the forest, feeling as though she had been transported to another time, another world.

Raven found herself surrounded by a large gathering of tribal people, gathered around a roaring fire with the mouthwatering scent of smoking salmon filling the air. The atmosphere was thick with tension and uncertainty, as everyone was acutely aware of the weighty decision that lay ahead. Raven's attention was drawn to a group of US government officials who stood before her, dressed in formal attire and adorned with hats and badges. They stood in a straight line, holding a large paper which Raven recognized as the Medicine Creek Treaty. The small cursive writing was illegible in the flickering firelight. Raven couldn't shake the feeling of nervousness as she stood before the solemn-faced officials. Their stern expressions and formal attire made her feel small and insignificant, like she was being judged by people from a different era. She couldn't help but notice how they resembled the historical figures she had read about in her textbooks, yet they also seemed strangely familiar, like everyday people dressed up in old-fashioned uniforms. The weight of their gaze bore down on her, and Raven couldn't help but wonder what they were thinking as they stared back at her. It was clear that this was a moment of great importance, one that would have a lasting impact on her people and their future. Raven could feel her heart beating rapidly in her chest as she tried to prepare herself for what was to come. She watched as her ancestors listened intently to the words being spoken, trying to understand the consequences of what was being proposed. Raven saw the faces of the elders, their expressions a mix of sadness, uncertainty, anger, and resignation. She saw the determination in the eyes of the warriors and medicine women, who were ready to fight to protect their people and their way of life. She felt the fear and uncertainty of the young ones, who didn't fully comprehend what was happening but knew that something big was about to change. As the officials finished speaking, Raven saw her ancestors slowly approach the paper, their hands shaking slightly as they signed X's on the page. She felt a surge of emotion as she realized the gravity of what they had just done - giving up their land, their freedom, and their way of life in exchange for promises that might not be kept. Raven couldn't move, she couldn't speak. She just stood watching the firelight dance on the kids' faces, and feeling the density of unease in the air.

Raven awoke with a start. "Ooh!" she cried, "that was intense."

As she sat up, Raven could still feel the vivid images of the dream lingering in her mind. She took a deep breath, trying to shake off the emotions that had been stirred up. It was hard to imagine the kind of pressure and uncertainty that her ancestors must have felt when they signed the Medicine Creek Treaty. Raven looked up at the cedar tree, feeling a renewed sense of appreciation and respect for the stories it had shared with her. She knew that there was so much more to learn and understand about her heritage, but for now, she was grateful for the small glimpse she had been given.

With a sigh, Raven rose to her feet and dusted off her clothes, feeling a newfound sense of calm wash over her. As she glanced around at the breathtaking scenery surrounding her, the golden rays of the setting sun painted the water in shimmering hues of orange and pink. But amidst the beauty, a pang of guilt tugged at Raven's heart as she thought of her family. They must be worried sick by now, she realized. The day had slipped away without a single text from her, and she hadn't shown up for school as expected. The impending darkness served as a stark reminder of the time that had passed, urging Raven to make her way back home before it was too late.

Raven's heart sank as she quickly grabbed her phone and saw several missed calls and texts from her mom and dad. She felt guilty for not checking in with them earlier. Raven quickly typed out a message to let them know she was okay and headed back towards the trail that would take her home.

As Raven was about to leave, the unexpected sound of the cedar tree's voice caught her off guard, causing her to freeze in place. "I have one last tale to share," the tree said solemnly, "but it will take many hours to tell. Before I begin, you must build a fire here, for the story I am about to impart requires the warmth and light of a flame. Once the tale is told, it will be yours to carry with you as you navigate through this world."

Raven hesitated, torn between her sense of duty to her worried family and her deep curiosity to hear the cedar's final tale. After a moment of contemplation, she made a decision. Pulling out her phone, she quickly sent a reassuring message to her parents, letting them know that she was safe but that she would be delayed a little longer. There was something important she needed to attend to first. Turning back to the cedar tree, Raven set her resolve and began to gather the necessary materials for a fire. Despite the encroaching darkness, she felt a sense of purpose and determination wash over her as she prepared to embark on this final journey with the wise old tree.

Raven's face lit up with a smile as she recalled her past experiences at the Vashon Wilderness

Program. The program had helped her connect to nature, and build skills in surviving and thriving in the forest. Building a fire was one of those skills. She had never been more grateful for the knowledge she had gained during her time there. As the light began to fade, Raven stood up and scanned the area for suitable materials to start the fire.

Raven recalled that the inner bark of cedar trees makes excellent tinder and began searching for some that had fallen to the ground. With a sharp rock, she scraped off some powdery dust to use as kindling, and gathered hemlock for fuel. She then broke small cedar branches and constructed a wooden tent around the kindling to protect it from the wind. With her attention to detail, she made sure to leave enough space for the air to circulate and feed the flames. As she worked, Raven's squinted eyes darted back and forth, taking in every detail of her surroundings.

She scanned the area for larger sticks and logs to use for fuel. After finding the right pieces, she carefully stripped off the bark to expose the driest part of the wood. With the fire structure complete, Raven's focus turned to gathering as much wood as possible before the daylight completely vanished.

She ran through the forest, collecting sticks and logs of all sizes, making sure she had enough to last as long as the story took. Huffing and wheezing, her arms filled with logs, she made her way from the fire to the forest. Back and forth she went until her cheeks grew pink and her forehead became damp. Finally, with a large pile of wood at her side, Raven sat back, satisfied with her work. She pulled out the matches from her pocket, smiling to herself that she had trusted her intuition earlier to grab them, and struck one on a rock. Then she carefully held it to the cedar scrapings and the hemlock at the center of the structure. As it grew, she stared at the fire, watching the flames dance and flicker, casting a warm glow across her face. She felt confident and capable, ready to listen to one more story.

As Raven gazed intently into the mesmerizing flames, she heard a deep voice resonating from the cedar tree.

The story of our people is not bound by a straight concept of time. Time is circular and interconnected. In the moments closer to our present journey, there were people with white skin and blue eyes who arrived on S'Homamish Island, renaming it Vashon. They saw the vast forests with abundant resources and began to cut us down for timber. They justified their power with their stories of greatness. Other towering trees, just as large and wise as I, were felled by the sharp metal tools they wielded. The trees carried some of the knowledge and stories of our people, and as they fell, it sank into the soil, decaying into the mushrooms and decomposers of the earth.

The once fallen forests eventually gave way to strawberry farms, and Vashon Island became known for producing some of the largest and tastiest strawberries around. The ancestor trees had nourished the soil. In fact, a Strawberry Festival was established and is still celebrated to this day. Through this festival, along with the farms and small businesses created by the island's inhabitants, a sense of community was fostered, with love and laughter helping to nourish the land. However, those farms were eventually disbanded due to the events of World War II.

The government forcibly removed Japanese-Americans who lived here on the island from their homes and sent them to internment camps, where they were stripped of their possessions and rights. This fear and chaos eroded some of the community bonds that had been formed on the island."

The tree sighed, as if remembering the moments not so long ago.

Despite the changes that have occurred on Vashon Island over the years, the legacy of the indigenous people still lives on. Their connection to the land and the natural world is deeply ingrained in the island's history and culture. Many people on Vashon work to honor this connection by working to pre-serve the island's beauty and promote nature connection. In my long life, I have stood wit-ness to the changing tides of Vashon's history. I have seen the forests fall and the straw-berry fields grow, only to be replaced by a new generation of artists and creatives. And yet, amidst all of these changes, the island remains a special and unique place with a strong sense of community and connection to the land.

The cedar paused, to let the words sink in. When it was ready it started speaking slowly.

What is most important is that all these people are a part of this island community. They care for each other and for the land. They work together to keep Vashon a beautiful and vibrant place. And even though the island has changed over time, the people here still honor the legacy of the tribal people who are ever present in this land, and still living out lives on Vashon, like you. As you sit here before me, Raven, I see the same connection to the land and nature that the tribal people had. Your willingness to learn and listen is a testament to the resilience and strength of the human spirit. The changes that have occurred on Vashon Island are a reflection of the ebb and flow of life, but it is through our connection to the land and to each other that we can find stability and purpose. The legacy of the tribal people lives on in the stories held by those who care, and in the natural beauty that surrounds us. It is up to each of us to carry on this legacy by preserving the land, respecting the natural world, and cultivating a strong sense of community. For it is in these things that we find the true meaning of life and the richness of our shared experiences. These experiences and connections to the land, to our ancestors, and to each other are what shape us and give us meaning. It is through reflection and remembrance that we can honor these connections and sow the seeds for a better world, one that we would be proud to be an ancestor of.

The cedar fell silent, its message delivered with a sense of wisdom and gravity.

As Raven thought about what the wise cedar tree had said, she started to really appreciate her island community and how they were connected to the land.

"A world I'd be proud to be an ancestor of," she quietly repeated those words to herself, trying to figure out what they meant. But thinking about it made her a bit confused. What did it mean to be proud of the world she'd be an ancestor of? What kind of world was that, anyway? Raven knew it wasn't a simple answer, and this question would stick with her for a long time.

The cedar tree must have sensed Raven's confusion because it spoke up again, in a kind and wise way. "Being proud of the world you'd be an ancestor of isn't something with clear rules," it explained. "It's a journey that lasts your whole life, Raven. The answer will show itself over time as you keep connecting with the land and the people around you. It's not about making a perfect world, but about working towards a world that's more complete than the one we got. It's like planting seeds for a good future, even if we don't know exactly what that future will be."

Raven's eyes got big as she realized what the cedar tree was saying. She felt a weight lift off her shoulders because she understood that making the world better wasn't a simple job. It was a tough and ongoing journey that needed patience, not giving up, and staying strong. She let out a big sigh, feeling better because it was okay not to have all the answers right away. Raven grinned, feeling like she had a fresh sense of purpose and determination in her heart.

Sitting quietly by the fading glow of her fire, Raven couldn't help but let her mind wander back to the adventure she had on her quest to find the cedar tree. The memory of navigating through the darkness and facing obstacles along the way was still fresh in her thoughts. But what stuck with her even more was the strong belief that something important was waiting for her, a belief that fueled her determination to keep going. As she pondered, Raven realized that the path ahead might hold similar challenges and moments of uncertainty, and she found herself thinking,

"Maybe that's okay."

The fire flickered and died, leaving Raven in the dark, but she knew that the light of the stars above would guide her on her journey. And now, as she looked up at the towering cedar tree, Raven knew that this was just the beginning of her journey. She knew that there would be more obstacles to overcome, more challenges to face, and more lessons to learn. But she was ready for the journey, fueled by her faith and her desire to create a better world, one that she would be proud to be an ancestor of. With a deep sense of gratitude and respect, Raven bowed her head to the cedar tree, acknowledging the wisdom and guidance it had provided. She took a deep breath and turned to face the cedar tree.

"Thank you for sharing all of these stories with me," she said, placing a gentle kiss on the bark of the tree. She recalled the moment earlier in the day when she had seen the cedar tree looking longingly at the water. Raven wanted to do something kind in return, to show her appreciation for the tree's wisdom and generosity.

"I have an idea," Raven said, her eyes shining bright with excitement. "How about I gather some of your cones and bring them to the water? I can plant your seeds in the soft soil near the shore as a gift for everything you've shared with me."

The cedar tree responded by rustling its branches, a gesture that Raven interpreted as a sign of agreement. A warm smile spread across her face, and she felt a burst of joy in her heart. Raven knew that planting the cedar's seeds was a small gesture, but it held deep meaning. It was a way to honor the special connection she felt with the tree and a commitment to carrying on the legacy of the tribal people. The cedar tree seemed to radiate gratitude as it replied.

"That would be a wonderful gift, Raven," the cedar tree replied with gratitude. "It would be an honor to have my descendants grow and spread their roots along the shore, close to the water that sustains us all."

With a determined nod, Raven set to work, gathering cones from the forest floor to plant near the cedar tree. Each cone represented a future generation of trees, a legacy of wisdom and connection to the land. Finally, she approached the altar and carefully plucked the last cone, the one that had been resting there all along. Tenderly, she kissed the cedar tree goodbye, feeling a sense of bittersweet farewell. As Raven turned to leave, the distant call of a raven echoed through the forest, a comforting reminder that she was on the right path. With a smile, she took a moment to savor the sound before setting off up the hill toward her bike. The darkness enveloped her as she pedaled homeward, but her heart was light with the knowledge that she would continue striving to be a good ancestor.

As Raven pedaled through the moonlit streets, the weight of the cedar cones seemed to grow heavier with each stroke of her bike. Anticipation and excitement pulsed through her veins, mingling with a sense of responsibility for the precious gift she held in her hands. With each passing moment, she drew closer to home, her heart racing with a mixture of emotions. Finally, she reached her doorstep and dismounted her bike, the cones cradled carefully in her arms. As she approached the door, she could hear the muffled sounds of voices inside, tinged with worry and impatience.

With a deep breath, Raven pushed open the door, revealing the worried faces of her parents waiting on the other side. Their eyes widened in surprise as they took in the sight of Raven standing before them, a determined look on her face and a bundle of cedar cones in her arms. Relief flooded their features, but it was tempered with a hint of frustration at her unexpected absence. Raven met their gaze with a mixture of apology and excitement, her heart pounding with the weight of her decision.

"Raven!" exclaimed her mother, her voice laced with worry. "Where have you been? We've been waiting here, scared out of our minds. Your text only made us more worried."

"Yeah, we have been calling the whole town looking for you," added her dad, his tone stern, eyebrows furrowed.

Raven hesitated, the words caught in her throat. "I was with the cedar tree down by the south cliff. It shared something important with me, and I wanted to plant its seeds as a thank you."

Her mom's eyes widened, a flicker of recognition in them. "The cedar tree? I've been there, too, Raven. But that was a long time ago. Why didn't you tell us where you were going?"

Raven sighed, frustration creeping into her voice, "I didn't think you'd understand, Mom. It's not just a tree; it's like a wise old friend. And I needed to do something to show my gratitude."

Her dad's frustration grew. "Raven, we need to know where you are. We can't have you disappearing without a word. It's not safe."

Raven, feeling a mix of defiance and frustration, shot back, "I'm not a little kid anymore! I can take care of myself. And I wanted to do something important, something that matters to us and our people."

Raven's mom's expression softened, a blend of understanding and concern flickering across her features. "Raven, we understand that you're growing up, but we still need to know where you are," she said gently. "And the cedar tree is special to me, too. I wish you had told us about your plans."

Raven's words hung in the air, carrying with them a sense of remorse. "I'm sorry, Mom, Dad," she said, her voice tinged with sincerity. "I didn't mean to worry you so much. But planting these seeds is important to me. It's like giving back to the tree that's given me so much."

Her parents exchanged a glance, their expressions softening with understanding. "We know, Raven," her dad said, his tone gentle. "And we appreciate your connection to nature. But next time, please remember to keep us informed. We just want to make sure you're safe."

Raven nodded, her heart heavy with regret for causing her parents concern. "I will, Dad," she promised, her voice filled with determination. "I'll make sure to communicate better from now on."

Her parents exchanged glances, a mixture of relief and concern lingering in the air. With a sense of resolution, Raven hugged her parents tightly, grateful for their understanding and support.

"Alright, kiddo," her dad said, giving her a reassuring pat on the back. "Let's talk about this more tomorrow. It's late, and we all need some rest."

The following morning the sun kissed the sky, signaling the start of a new day. The aroma of breakfast wafted through the air as Raven's family gathered in the cozy kitchen. The table was set with a variety of morning delights—granola, eggs and some toast.

Raven's little sister, Naya, with an exaggerated pout, couldn't resist teasing her, "Raven, you seriously ate all the Lucky Charms? Now we're stuck with the boring granola. Ugh!"

Her younger brother Kai, joined in, shaking his head in mock disappointment, "Come on, Raven! The cereal monster strikes again! What are we going to do without our Lucky Charms?"

Raven rolled her eyes, a mix of amusement

and mild frustration playing on her face. "Hey, I needed all the luck I could get for my adventures. And they're not just charms, they're power-ups!"

Curiosity danced in her siblings' eyes as they devoured their breakfast. Between bites of scrambled eggs, Naya asked, "Hey, Raven, where have you been disappearing off to lately? Are you on some secret mission or something?"

Kai chimed in, "Yeah, spill the beans, Raven! What's going on?"

Raven chuckled, a mischievous glint in her eye. "Well, I've been hanging out with the cedar tree down by the cliff. It's been sharing stories with me, and I've been planting its seeds as a way of saying thank you."

Her siblings exchanged curious glances, and Naya raised an eyebrow. "A talking tree? Seriously?"

"Seriously," Raven replied with a grin. "And it's not just any tree; it's like a wise old friend with lots of stories to tell."

Her siblings couldn't contain their curiosity. Between bites of pancakes, they bombarded her with questions.

"Come on, Raven, spill the details! What kind of stories is this cedar tree telling you?" Naya demanded.

Raven grinned, savoring a moment of suspense before sharing, "Well, it told me about the orca, the thunderbird, and the salmon. There are these incredible stories about our people and the spirits of the land and sea. Like, did you know that the orca used to be a human and got transformed into a sea creature to protect and guide our ancestors?"

Kai's eyes widened with amazement. "No way! That's like a real-life superhero origin story!"

"Exactly!" Raven nodded. "And the thunderbird is this powerful symbol of strength and courage, guarding us from harm. It's like our own guardian spirit."

Naya chimed in, "And what about the salmon? What's their story?"

Raven's eyes sparkled. "The salmon represents the cycles of nature and the bounty of the land and sea. It's a sacred being, and our people catch them with their bare hands, nets, and hooks, honoring their spirit and strength."

As Raven finished recounting the stories from the cedar tree, a newfound sense of connection lingered in the room. Her family sat captivated by the rich tales that echoed with the spirit of their people.

With a glint in her eye, Raven turned to her family and said, "I have these cedar cones, and I want to plant the seeds by the water as a way of giving back to the cedar tree. It's like passing on the wisdom and connection we've gained."

Kai grinned, "That sounds awesome! Can we come, too?"

"Yeah, Raven, count us in!" added Naya excitement dancing in her eyes.

Raven's parents exchanged knowing smiles and nodded in agreement. "It sounds like a meaningful way to spend the day together," her mom said.

Her dad chimed in, "Let's make it a family outing. We can share the experience and create a deeper connection to our heritage."

As they finished their breakfast, Raven's dad took out his phone. "I'll give the school a call and let them know you all won't be coming in today. We're taking a family day to connect with our roots."

Determined to fulfill her promise to the cedar tree, Raven and her family eagerly made their way down to the water, the cedar cones cradled in her hands. The familiar scent of saltwater filled the air as Raven reached the shore. Her parents joined her, their expressions a blend of curiosity and support, while

Naya and Kai, sensing the importance of the moment, skipped along, excitement radiating from their faces.

Together, they selected a spot near the water's edge, soft soil beneath their fingers. Raven carefully planted the cedar cones, pressing them gently into the earth. The grains of soil clung to her fingers as if whispering secrets to the seeds below. Her parents watched in silence, recognizing the significance of the act, while her younger siblings gazed with wide-eyed wonder at the unfolding ceremony.

"There you go, little ones," Raven whispered, a smile playing on her lips. "Grow strong, just like the cedar tree, and connect our roots to this land."

Kai and Naya, though young, mimicked Raven's actions, gently patting the soil around the seeds. Her parents, understanding the profoundness of the moment, placed their hands on Raven's shoulders. The family stood together, for a moment of stillness, as the sun continued its ascent in the sky.

After planting the cedar cones, Raven and her family decided to celebrate the moment with some play by the water. Kai and Naya eagerly splashed in the shallows, laughter bubbling up as the cool waves tickled their feet.

Amidst the playful splashes and shared laughter, Naya suddenly paused, her eyes narrowing mischievously. "Hey, Raven," she teased, "remember when you ate all the Lucky Charms yesterday? Now there are none left!"

Raven chuckled, a playful glint in her eyes. "Guilty as charged, little sis. I'll make it up to you somehow."

Kai chimed in, adding to the playful banter, "Maybe Raven can use her magic powers to make Lucky Charms rain from the sky!"

Raven smiled and grabbed a rock, throwing it with all her might into the water. Kai clapped his hands, his excitement contagious. "Nice throw, Raven! Bet you can't hit that big rock over there!"

Challenge accepted, Raven playfully raised an eyebrow and picked up a smooth, flat stone. She gauged the distance, squinting her eyes in mock concentration, and then executed a skilled throw. The stone sailed through the air, gracefully arcing toward the distant rock. A satisfying "Splash!" followed as the stone hit its mark.

Naya's laughter bubbled up, contagious and joyful, as she reached for her own colorful pebble. With a mischievous grin, she flung it into the water, creating a playful splash that sent droplets sparkling in the sunlight. Inspired by her sister's enthusiasm, Kai and Raven joined in, their pebbles skipping across the surface in a spirited dance. Their parents watched with smiles, their hearts warmed by the simple joy of their children's laughter. Encouraged by their parents' presence, the family engaged in a friendly rock-throwing competition, each member trying to outdo the others with splashes of increasing artistry. Laughter filled the air, mingling with the rhythmic symphony of rocks meeting water, creating a harmonious moment of shared delight and familial connection.

Raven's mom, relishing the family's playful moments by the water, suddenly noticed a group of tourists approaching the shore with buckets, seemingly ready to gather clams. As Raven's mom waded through the gentle waves toward the group of approaching tourists, her concern etched across her face like ripples on the water's surface.

"Hello," she greeted them with a warm smile, though her eyes held a firmness. "I hope you're enjoying your time here. I just wanted to check in with you, do you have a permit for collecting shellfish in this area?"

The tourists glanced at one another, a bit surprised by the question. One of them hesitated before replying, "Uh, no, we didn't know we needed one."

Raven's mom nodded understandingly, her expression softening with empathy. "I understand it can be confusing," she said gently. "But it's important to ensure that we're following the regulations set in place to protect our coastal ecosystems. Without proper permits, harvesting shellfish can disrupt the delicate balance of marine life and damage the environment."

"See, these shores are really special to us," Raven's mom said, pointing around. "We're allowed to fish and gather shellfish here because it's part of our heritage, protected by agreements. It's also important to be respectful on public lands and follow the ways of the indigenous people. Not being respectful can hurt communities like ours."

She continued, her tone firm yet patient, "It's really important to know and follow the rules in the area and show respect for the land. If you want to gather shellfish, make sure you ask the people in charge and get the right permissions. This helps keep nature healthy and respects the rights of the native people."

She paused, giving the tourists a moment to absorb her words before continuing, "Luckily, there are resources available to help you navigate these guidelines. I'd be happy to point you in the right direction or provide more information if you'd like."

The tourists listened carefully, their eyes wide with surprise as Raven's mom explained the importance of protecting the shoreline and its inhabitants. With a nod, they acknowledged their mistake, promising to be more mindful in the future. Raven's mom approached her family with a content smile. "Well, that went well," she said, settling down on the sand beside them.

"Yeah, Mom, you really showed them," Kai chimed in, his eyes gleaming with admiration.

Naya nodded enthusiastically. "You're like a superhero, Mom!"

Raven added, "I saw those people earlier this week, I didn't know what to do. I'm really glad you told them what's up."

Her mom chuckled, her cheeks tinged with a hint of pink. "Thanks, kiddos. But remember, standing up for what's right is something we can all do, no matter how big or small."

Raven grinned, feeling proud of her mom's bravery. "You're awesome," she said, giving her a supportive pat on the back.

As the sun dipped lower on the horizon, casting a golden hue over the tranquil scene, Raven's family settled into a comfortable silence, enjoying the peaceful rhythm of the waves. They watched as seabirds skimmed the water's surface and the occasional seal popped up to say hello.

Naya broke the quietude with a sudden burst of energy. "Let's build a sandcastle!" she exclaimed, her eyes sparkling with excitement.

Kai jumped up, eager to join in the fun. "Yeah, let's make it the biggest one ever!"

Raven grinned, already envisioning their masterpiece. "I'll gather some shells for decoration," she volunteered, bounding off along the shoreline.

The sun dipped lower in the sky, casting a warm glow across the shore. The laughter of her siblings echoed, a sweet melody harmonizing with the rhythmic lapping of the waves.

As the seeds nestled snugly into the rich soil, Raven felt a deep sense of connection not just to the cedar tree, but to her family and the island itself. The ancient stories woven into the fabric of their lives seemed to echo through the gentle rustle of the wind, binding them together in a tapestry of heritage and tradition. With each passing moment, the tensions of the day melted away, replaced by a profound sense of unity and belonging. As they stood together on the shoreline, Raven's family felt the weight of history and the promise of the future intertwine, anchoring them to the land and to each other.

As the family gathered their belongings to head back home, Raven's mom put a hand on her shoulder, the glow of the setting sun reflecting in her eyes.

"Thank you, Raven," she said, her voice filled with sincerity. "For reminding us of the importance of our heritage and connection to the land. It's easy to forget in the hustle and bustle of everyday life, but moments like these bring it all back into focus."

Raven's heart swelled with a deep sense of pride and excitement as she reflected on the day's events. Each moment felt like a thread weaving together the tapestry of her heritage, unraveling the mysteries of the tribal people who had called this island home for generations. With each step she took, the island seemed to come alive, its secrets whispering through the rustling leaves and the gentle lapping of the waves. As the sun dipped lower in the sky, casting a golden hue over the landscape, Raven's thoughts turned to the last remaining cedar cone nestled in her pocket. It felt heavy with significance.

With a determined nod, Raven approached the spot where she had found the red stone, a sense of reverence washing over her as she knelt down. Placing the cedar cone in the earth, she whispered a silent prayer, feeling the weight of her ancestors' presence surrounding her.

Suddenly, a soft murmur on the wind caught Raven's attention, causing her to furrow her brow in confusion. She hadn't realized that the cedar tree could speak to her without the red stone in her pocket. Yet, there it was, a gentle reassurance echoing through the air, reminding her of the importance of her actions.

Raven's mom noticed her daughter's solemn expression and approached her with a gentle smile. "What are you doing, Raven?"

Raven looked up, her eyes reflecting the fading light of the setting sun. "I'm planting the last cedar cone," she replied, her voice tinged with determination. "The cedar tree spoke to me, Mom. It said I'm being a good ancestor."

Her mom's eyes widened in surprise, but then softened with understanding. "That's wonderful, Raven," she said, placing a hand on her daughter's shoulder. "I'm proud of you."

Raven nodded, a sense of peace settling over her. "Thanks, Mom," she said, her voice filled with gratitude. "I just want to do what's right for our family and our island."

As they watched Raven carefully plant the cone in the earth, her siblings gathered around, their curious eyes reflecting the fading light. "What are you doing, Raven?" asked Kai, his voice filled with curiosity.

"I'm planting the last cedar cone," Raven explained, her voice steady with purpose. "The cedar tree told me to."

Naya nodded in understanding, her young face serious. "That's important, Raven," she said, her voice soft but determined. "We have to take care of the island."

Raven smiled at her siblings, feeling a surge of pride in their shared commitment to their home. "Yeah," she agreed, her voice echoing with determination. "We have to take care of each other, too."

With a final push, Raven gently pressed the cone into the earth, feeling a sense of fulfillment wash over her. As the last rays of sunlight faded into the horizon, she knew that she was carrying on the legacy of her ancestors and shaping the future of her family and her island home.

As Raven and her family walked along the sandy shore, the distant cry of seagulls echoed in the evening air. The sky was painted with hues of orange and pink as the sun dipped below the horizon, casting a warm glow over the landscape. With each step, Raven felt a sense of peace wash over her, knowing that she had honored her ancestors and taken a step towards shaping the future of her island home.

As they neared the edge of the beach, a sudden gust of wind swept through the trees, carrying with it the faint whisper of the cedar tree's voice. Raven's heart skipped a beat as she turned back, searching for any sign of the ancient cedar. But all she saw was the lapping waves and the fading light.

With a bittersweet smile, Raven knew that her time with the cedar tree had come to an end. But in its place was a newfound sense of purpose and determination. As the stars began to twinkle overhead, she felt a surge of hope for the future, knowing that the legacy of her ancestors would live on in her heart and in the hearts of her family.

As Raven's family piled into the car, ready to head home for dinner, a lone raven called out in the night, its haunting cry echoing through the darkness. Raven paused for a moment, her gaze drawn to the sky where the silhouette of the bird danced against the backdrop of twinkling stars.

"It's like the cedar tree is saying goodbye," she whispered to herself, a sense of melancholy tugging at her heartstrings.

As the car moved into the darkness of the night, a single star twinkled above, its light piercing through the sky. Naya and Kai pressed their faces against the window, their breath fogging the glass as they gazed up at the celestial wonder.

"Look! A shooting star!" Naya exclaimed, her voice filled with excitement. "Quick, let's make a wish!"

Kai nodded eagerly, closing his eyes tightly as he made his wish. Naya followed suit, her lips moving silently as she sent her hopes into the night.

Raven smiled at their innocence, her heart warmed by their belief in the magic of the universe. And as she glanced up at the star, a silent wish formed in her mind. She wished for more adventures, more moments of wonder and discovery with her family by her side. Somehow, she knew it would happen.

With their wishes whispered into the night, the car continued on its journey, the faint light of the star guiding them forward. And with each passing moment, Raven felt a renewed sense of excitement and anticipation for the adventures that lay ahead.

Made in the USA
Monee, IL
12 November 2024

69479280R00065